NATURE'S SCALES

Weighing Environmental Issues

Maureen Mecozzi

Contents

Rigby

THE ENVIRONMENT:
A tricky balance

Mention the **environment** and you will probably hear as many strong opinions as there are people in the room. Why do people care so much about nature—Earth's land, water, air, and animals? It's because nature offers so much. It provides resources for food, homes, employment, recreation, transportation, and more.

There is another reason why the environment sparks heated discussions. Earth's growing population means that ways must be found to share the planet's **natural resources** with other humans and with animals. Sharing is a fine policy, but in practice, it can be difficult. Everyone has a different idea about how resources should be divided.

This book includes four sections, each focusing on a different environmental issue. First you will read a brief description of the issue and what it means. Then you will read two different viewpoints on the matter.

As you read, consider the arguments offered in support of each viewpoint. In any debate about the environment, you will find many facts and an equal amount of emotion. Sometimes the same fact can be used to support a claim on both sides. It all depends on how the information is presented or interpreted. As you read, think about each issue and your own feelings on the matter. Then consider which side you would take in a debate.

GRIZZLIES:
Bring them back or let them go?

What is the issue?

In stories of the Old West, cowboys often gathered around the campfire to sing an old tune:

Home, home on the range,
where the deer and the
antelope play . . .

In those days, there was another animal that roamed the plains and foothills of the Rocky Mountains. This animal was seldom mentioned in song. It was a creature that was both feared and respected by most people—the grizzly bear.

Grizzly bears once roamed freely throughout central Idaho and western Montana. When settlers began moving into the region in the 1800s, they brought **livestock** with them. To

the bears, these herds of sheep, cattle, and horses were easy prey.

Of course, the settlers did not want their costly animals to become grizzly food. So they began to kill any bears that came close to their livestock. They also killed some that did not. In fact, by the 1930s, the grizzly bear was no longer seen in the region.

This didn't happen just in Idaho and Montana. By 1975, there were very few grizzly bears left in the **continental U.S.** and the animals were on the threatened list. Because of its threatened status, the grizzly fell under the protection of the Endangered Species Act. This law directs the federal government to take action in order to protect species whose numbers have dropped.

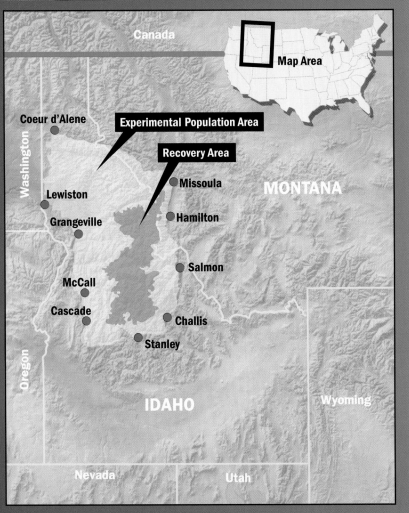

The Selway-Bitterroot Wilderness area is highlighted.

The U.S. Fish and Wildlife Service now plans to bring grizzly bears back to Idaho and Montana, to the Selway-Bitterroot Wilderness, which includes parts of eastern Idaho and western Montana. Scientists and environmentalists say that bears are necessary to restore the balance of nature in that region.

But some ranchers and residents close to the area are against the reintroduction of the grizzly. They say the bears will again prey on livestock, and they fear that people won't want to spend time in the wilderness if they have to share it with bears.

Should the grizzly bear be returned to the wilderness? Read on to learn about two different viewpoints on the matter. Then consider how you feel about the issue.

In the continental U.S., fewer than 1,000 grizzly bears now occupy less than 1 percent of the land they originally roamed.

A vote **FOR** the grizzlies

What is a wilderness without one of its wildest creatures, the grizzly bear? It is estimated that in the early 1800s there were almost 100,000 grizzlies roaming North America. Today, the grizzly population is less than half that. Grizzlies have nearly been eliminated everywhere in the United States except Alaska. In fact, in the continental U.S., fewer than 1,000 bears now occupy less than 1 percent of the land they originally roamed.

To environmentalists, this is a warning. The grizzly bear is an "indicator species." That means it serves as a measure of the environment's health in a particular location. When an indicator species is in trouble, it means the entire **ecosystem** is out of balance.

Supporters of reintroducing the grizzly say the animals help the wilderness habitat. By preying on sick animals, grizzly bears help to keep deer, bison, and other animal populations healthy and strong. Bears also spread seeds from the plants they eat. If there are no grizzly bears left to play these roles, countless other species may suffer.

Those in favor of reintroducing the grizzly also point out that the odds of being attacked by a bear are slim. In fact, biologists say the chance is one in a million. In wilderness areas, more people die from drowning, climbing accidents, and heart failure than from grizzly attacks. Supporters of grizzlies feel that the benefits of returning the species to a small part of its former habitat far outweigh the risks.

One important reason for the grizzlies' decline has been the loss of their natural habitat. Because of their large size, grizzlies consume a lot of food. They can eat 80 to 90 pounds of food per day during their peak eating period—summer to early fall. Grizzlies are omnivorous—they eat both meat and plants. But since they eat so much, they need a large area in which to hunt.

In many places, it is difficult for grizzlies to find enough food, because humans have

changed the landscape. Towns, highways, and railroads have cut the bears' natural range into smaller and smaller sections. Activities such as logging, mining, ranching, and tourism have further changed the grizzlies' feeding grounds. It is almost impossible to keep the bears from crossing human boundaries and coming into contact with people.

Environmentalists and scientists are convinced that there is only one way to save this magnificent animal. It must have a home in the wilderness away from people. Rather than protecting people from grizzlies, efforts should be made to protect the grizzlies from people.

A vote ~~AGAINST~~ the grizzlies

Let's face it: The grizzly is not your average bear. These enormous creatures can weigh as much as 1,500 pounds. A mature grizzly can run at speeds of up to 35 miles per hour—much faster than the fastest human runner. Grizzlies have jaws and teeth that are capable of snapping a pine tree in half. They have strong upper limbs and 6-inch claws. A grizzly can kill a moose, elk, or buffalo with a single swipe of its powerful paws.

It's no surprise, then, that some people say that grizzly bears should be kept as far away from humans as possible. One Idaho resident claims that bringing the bear back is like "introducing sharks at the beach."

Some people see nothing wrong with letting the grizzly bear become **extinct**. They say that extinction is a natural process and should not be interfered with. They point out that the vast majority of species that have ever lived on Earth are now extinct.

Biologists say grizzly bears are naturally wary of people. But statistics indicate otherwise. Bears have killed several dozen backpackers and hunters in North America in the past century. In 1998, there were 263 confirmed human-grizzly encounters in the western United States. This is an all-time record. More than half of these incidents took place in developed areas near homes, and not in the forest or mountains.

Clearly, the bears that do still live in the West have become used to people. As the bears lose their fear of humans, there is more chance for trouble. Why make the problem worse by bringing more bears back to the area?

Hungry bears will attack livestock. This has been happening ever since people established sheep and cattle ranches close to the bears' habitat. Some ranchers have reported losing six or seven animals a night to grizzlies. Naturally, the loss of expensive livestock is an economic problem for these ranchers.

Certainly there are things communities and ranchers can do to discourage bears. One idea is to install bright lights around livestock pens. Another is to keep ranches, towns, and campgrounds clean and free of garbage. Still, the issue remains: bears are bears and people are people. The two just don't mix.

Bear Country

All Wildlife Is Dangerous
Do Not Approach Or Feed

CITIES:
Growing places or wide-open spaces?

⬤ What is the issue?

America has changed greatly in the last 55 years. Between 1945 and 2000, the U.S. population rose from 133 million to 281.4 million people. To serve the needs of this growing population, homes, schools, office buildings, and shopping malls have been built. They stand on land that was once forest, prairie, wetland, or farmland.

Many cities and towns across America continue to expand into outlying areas. This kind of rapid growth is called "**urban** sprawl."

Some people say there is no cause for worry—there is plenty of open land in the United States. They say

that developing the land is a sign of healthy growth. They feel that people should have the right to build homes and businesses wherever land is available.

Others believe that there is a need to preserve land for farming, wildlife **habitats**, and other **conservation** purposes. They say that the growth of cities and **suburbs** should be controlled.

On the following pages, you will read about two different viewpoints on community development. The people and the town are not real. However, the problems and decisions they face are. After reading, consider how you feel. Should this community's growth be limited or not?

For the past four years, Sally Jones has been the mayor of Urbandale, a community located in the eastern United States. Her ties to the city go back much further, though. Sally was born and raised in Urbandale. During her thirty-nine years, she has seen the city experience amazing growth.

"When I was ten, the town was like an island. It was all by itself in a sea of green," Sally said. "A beautiful pine forest bordered the northern edge of Urbandale. Owls and hawks used to nest there in the spring. South and east of town, there were grassy fields dotted with oak trees. They circled Cattail Pond, where we fished for bluegills when I was a kid. To the west, there were small farms and hay fields."

Back then, only a few thousand people lived in Urbandale. "But when folks saw what a nice town we had, they wanted to live here, too," said Sally. "People from a large city 40 miles northwest of Urbandale began buying small pieces of land and putting up houses—one here, one there."

Between 1945 and 2000, the U.S. population rose from 133 million to 281.4 million people.

By the time Sally was twenty years old, there were many new houses in Urbandale. Because the land was in demand, prices went up. Some farmers began to sell off large parcels of land. They could make more money that way than by farming. Before long, farming was no longer an important part of Urbandale's **economy**.

Many of the city's new residents were **commuters**. They drove to their jobs in the larger city, 40 miles away. Traffic became so bad that the state Transportation Department decided to build an expressway. "It was called Pine Highway, in honor of the forest it replaced," Sally recalled. "People said the new road took 10 minutes off their commute. That's nice for them, but not for the owls and hawks. Once the forest was gone, so were the birds."

The year Sally turned thirty-five, a developer bought large sections of Urbandale's remaining open space, including Cattail Pond. Hundreds

of new apartments were built and thousands of people moved in. The pond, once home to bluegills and cattails, was drained to become a golf course.

The increase in population brought many problems with it. Urbandale's **utility** companies struggled to provide enough water and electricity to the new homes. Added traffic meant that even with Pine Highway, roads were crowded with commuters. Before long, the once-clean air of Urbandale began to show signs of pollution.

That was the last straw for Sally. She was upset by the rapid changes taking place. She was concerned about the loss of the city's beautiful natural features. So Sally decided to do something about it. She ran for mayor of Urbandale on a no-growth **platform** and won by a narrow margin. "Urbandale has been swallowed whole," she said. "There is nothing but houses, highways, and businesses between here and the big city. And what's happening here is happening all around the country. In the United States, the amount of land that has changed from **rural** to urban use has risen steadily. We don't want any more of that kind of growth here in Urbandale."

Sally has promised to stop development. She wants to restore forested areas and open spaces, and bring back a "small-town feeling." The job will not be easy. A proposal for a new six-lane expressway is before the city council. And the last remaining parcel of open land is due to become an **industrial park**.

A vote FOR growth

Sally's twin brother, Sam, has also lived in Urbandale all his life. As children, Sam and Sally loved to fish together in Cattail Pond. That memory and a fondness for Urbandale are about the only things the twins now share.

"There's no such thing as urban sprawl," says Sam. "What people like my sister call sprawl is really just growth. Growth is natural. It's necessary. Communities would fade away without it."

He remembers the old Urbandale as "a poky little town, without much to do or see." When Sam was young, Urbandale didn't have a movie theater or a bowling alley. There were no decent soccer fields or baseball diamonds. The nearest hospital was 40 miles away. The high school was small and

About 80 percent of the U.S. population now lives in urban regions. But these regions account for only about 3 percent of U.S. land.

its programs were limited. It didn't even have a science lab or a marching band.

What about Cattail Pond? "Sure, the fishing was fun," Sam says, "but everybody forgets about the horrible mosquitoes and the spring flooding."

Today's bustling Urbandale is more to Sam's liking. The city has well-equipped schools, a community recreation center, and a big library. There are many restaurants and shops and good medical facilities.

Sam is the director of Urbandale's Commerce Club. This organization was established to promote the city and attract new businesses and industries. The Commerce Club's most recent project is the industrial park proposal.

Sam and other members of the club worked hard to attract a buyer for the land. The businesses that are to be built there will help keep Urbandale's economy humming. "It's time that last weedy piece of land was put to good use," Sam says of the site. "New businesses in the industrial park will create jobs. And jobs provide money for our families."

Sam admits that more manufacturing means more chance of polluting Urbandale's groundwater and air. However, he feels this is a price that area residents are willing to pay. "You can't grow without making a little bit of a mess," he reasons. "Besides, there are lots of laws to control pollution, and new ways to clean up pollution are being discovered every year. So even if we have some problems, it's not like it'll be a permanent thing."

Sam is leading the Commerce Club's campaign for the new six-lane expressway. He knows good roads are necessary for continued growth. With better roads, more people will move to Urbandale. The town and its economy can continue to expand. "I've checked the **census** statistics," says Sam. "About 80 percent of the U.S. population now lives in urban regions. But these regions account for only about 3 percent of U.S. land. The way I see it, there's plenty of space here for everyone."

ZOOS:
Use them or lose them?

What is the issue?

Zoos have long been favorite places for people to observe exotic and unusual creatures. However, in recent years, zoos have changed. Instead of simply offering entertainment, zoos have become caretakers of Earth's **biodiversity**. Species whose populations have decreased in the wild are being raised in zoos. Some people believe zoos are the only answer to saving endangered animals from extinction and preserving them for future generations.

There is another side to consider, though. Zoo opponents say that the existence of zoos gives humans an excuse to further destroy forests, jungles, grasslands, and other natural habitats. They see zoos as animal prisons and believe caging wild creatures is wrong and cruel. In their opinion, zoos are things of the past that should be **abolished**.

Study the viewpoints of two very different public interest organizations. Then consider how you feel about this issue. Should we enjoy what zoos have to offer—or should we ban them?

Zoos have changed a lot since they first became popular nearly 200 years ago. In old-fashioned zoos, animals were often housed alone in barred or glassed-in cages. Spectators could "ooh" and "aah," but they learned little about how the animal lived in the wild.

In modern zoos, animals live in social groups in settings similar to their natural habitats. This is both healthier for the animals and more educational for visitors.

The World Zoo Organization (WZO) is a group dedicated to improving zoos around the globe. The WZO says several factors have contributed to the change in zoos. Over the years, humans have greatly increased their knowledge of life sciences. At the same time, rapid population growth, increased pollution, and the overuse of natural resources have threatened the survival of many animal species.

As a result, zoos are becoming conservation centers. Approximately one million animals are housed in the more than 1,000 zoos represented by the WZO. Many of those animals belong to species in danger of becoming extinct. By protecting these animals, zoos help protect the **diversity** of life.

Supporters of zoos point out that at least 14 species that have become extinct in the wild have been saved through zoo breeding programs. Several species, like the European bison and the Arabian oryx, have already been successfully reintroduced into the wild. Others, like the California condor, are in the early years of restoration. Still other species await improving conditions in what remains of their natural habitat.

According to estimates, nearly 600,000,000 people—approximately 10 percent of the world's population—visit zoos annually.

The WZO considers the condor to be a perfect example of the vital role zoos play. By 1985, only nine condors remained in the wild. On April 19, 1987, the last free-flying condor was placed in captivity. At that time, only 27 condors were in existence—all in zoos. Successful breeding programs at the San Diego and Los Angeles zoos resulted in a doubling of the condor population by 1992. Over time, some birds were released back into their natural habitat. Today there are 155 condors; 56 of them live in the wild.

According to estimates, nearly 600,000,000 people—approximately 10 percent of the world's population—visit zoos annually. During these visits, people not only have fun, but they also learn how nature's balance can be disturbed by humans. By showing how animals behave, adapt, eat, and grow, modern zoos can explain the connections between human activities and the survival of other species.

In addition, scientists use zoos as laboratories in which they can observe animals that are difficult to locate in the wild. Studying the behavior of animals in zoos may help scientists preserve wild species whose natural habitats are shrinking.

Zoo supporters point out the many important roles zoos play: education, protection of rare species, and the advancement of scientific knowledge. But they also stress another important aspect of the zoo. It is a unique place where people have the opportunity to spend time in the company of other creatures with whom they share the planet.

A vote AGAINST zoos

Throughout the world, there are many different types of zoos. They range from large city collections to small children's zoos, from aquariums to safari parks. All are designed for the entertainment of human visitors. Many even stage animal shows, with chimpanzees riding tricycles or seals balancing balls on their noses.

However, not everyone thinks these performances are harmless entertainment. The Born Free Foundation (BFF) wants to see an end to traditional zoos. The group does not agree with the claim that zoos play an important role in education, research, and conservation.

According to the BFF, a zoo is first and foremost a business. Zoos exist to make money, not to protect animals or educate the public. The foundation points to the tiger as an example of what zoos really do.

These fearsome cats are among the most popular of zoo residents. Having a tiger is a sure way to increase any zoo's ticket sales. To make sure there are enough big cats to go around, hundreds of tigers are born in zoos. In the wild, tiger cubs stay two years with their mothers, learning how to survive. In zoos, cubs are often separated from their mothers and sold shortly after birth.

To date, not one tiger has been reintroduced into the wild. This is despite the fact that several tiger species are on the endangered animal list. Zoos spend millions of dollars raising and exhibiting tigers. Zoo opponents say the money should be spent on efforts to protect wild tigers in their natural habitat.

Opponents also disagree with the claim that endangered animals should be kept alive in captivity until their wild habitat has been restored. They point to increasing evidence that animals raised in zoos from birth adapt to zoo life. They never develop the instincts and skills needed to survive in the wild.

The BFF even questions the role of zoos in education, especially in the case of elephants. In the wild, these social animals live in large family groups. However, zoos cannot provide the kind of space a family of elephants would need. So most zoos are limited to one or two elephants. Obviously, visitors cannot learn about the elephant's life in the wild by observing one or two of these magnificent creatures.

Many who oppose zoos are passionate about the issue of animal rights. They feel that it is wrong for animals to be bought, sold, and traded. They refer to research showing that animals have dreams and can remember sequences of events. They say any kind of zoo is wrong because the animals are still not free.

The point of view of zoo opponents is clear: animals should remain in their natural habitat. Efforts should focus on preserving these habitats in order to ensure the animals' survival.

WIND FARMS:
Pollution-free energy or a lot of hot air?

What is the issue?

No TV, no CD player, no cold soda pop in the refrigerator on a hot summer day. No heat or light to add comfort to a chilly winter night. Without electricity, the world would be a very different place.

However, producing electricity is not a small, inexpensive, or clean task. Coal and natural gas power plants create pollution. Nuclear plants produce dangerous radioactive waste. Hydroelectric plants block rivers and disrupt habitats for fish and wildlife.

But what if there was a way to produce electricity without causing any of these problems? A U.S. energy

company thinks it has the answer—
wind. This company says that wind
is a renewable, nonpolluting source
of energy. It wants to build a "wind
farm" near the small town of
Allenton, in southeastern Wisconsin.
Allenton is in one of the fastest-
growing areas in the state.

A wind farm is actually a group
of **turbines**. Each turbine is a tall
tower with what looks like a big
airplane propeller on top. These
modern-day windmills catch the
breeze and convert the motion of
the spinning blades into electricity.

Some citizens have formed a group
called Taxpayers for the Wind Farm.
Their purpose is to gather support
for the project. However, another

group has banded together as the local preservation group. This group believes that wind power is not as trouble-free as the energy company claims. They oppose putting a wind farm in the area. "Maybe it would be all right somewhere else," they say, "but not in my backyard."

Read the claims on both sides of this argument. Then consider for yourself: are wind farms a source of pollution-free energy, or are they a lot of hot air?

A vote **FOR** the wind farm

Currently, Wisconsin gets about 75 percent of its power from coal plants. As these plants operate, they pump pollutants into the air. According to estimates, in one year the plants pump out 48 million tons of carbon dioxide, 206,000 tons of sulfur dioxide, and 107,000 tons of nitrogen oxide. These gases are known to contribute to global warming, acid rain, and smog.

Wind farms could help clear the air. The wind farm near Allenton would have 28 wind turbines along a 5-mile stretch of hills. At the top of each 235-foot-tall tower, there would be three 90-foot-long blades to catch the wind. It would be the largest wind farm in the state.

Wisconsin produces no coal, oil, natural gas, or uranium. The state must spend over 6 billion dollars per year to buy these fuels. In addition, 15 percent of the electricity consumed in Wisconsin is purchased from out-of-state suppliers. Supporters of wind power say that depending so heavily on outside energy sources is costly and foolish. They ask: what will happen when these fuels are no longer available, as many scientists predict will happen?

According to the energy company, wind power is the answer. The company points out that wind is a source of energy that is always available and causes no pollution. It claims that its project could generate enough electricity to meet the needs of 6,000 homes. The wind farm turbines would be built and maintained locally, which would provide jobs for Wisconsin workers. Best of all, the electricity produced would be purchased and used by local consumers.

Some people have asked questions about noise. A turbine's spinning blades do make a swooshing, humming noise. People have compared the sound to waves pounding gently on a beach. The noise is something people become used to, says the company. It speaks from experience: the company owns more than a dozen wind farms in the United States.

The company also says that it will work to prevent any noise from bothering residents. Towers will be located at least 1,000 feet from homes. They will also be a minimum of 650 feet from any roads.

A wind farm is a good deal for the community, supporters insist. The landowners who rent space for the turbines will receive a steady source of income. The taxes the company pays will benefit the town's treasury. And electricity will be cheaper for local consumers.

Taxpayers for the Wind Farm know that people want the benefits of electricity. They also recognize that many of the same people do not want power generators in their backyards. However, they feel that having a wind farm is far better than having a coal or nuclear power plant in their community.

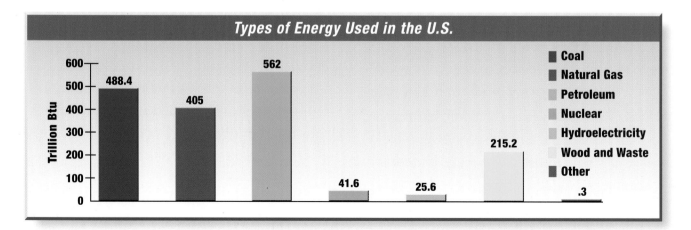

Types of Energy Used in the U.S.

Trillion Btu

Coal	488.4
Natural Gas	405
Petroleum	562
Nuclear	41.6
Hydroelectricity	25.6
Wood and Waste	215.2
Other	.3

A vote against the wind farm

What some people in Allenton see as a clean, renewable source of energy, others see as a potential problem. The huge wind towers on the proposed wind farm would be visible for 20 miles, say members of the preservation group. They maintain that the towers will spoil the country atmosphere with its gently rolling hills, small farms, woodlands, and clusters of houses.

The term "wind farm" is misleading, the group insists. It isn't a farm in the traditional sense, with green fields and tree-lined fences. A wind farm is a vast industrial site filled with big, noisy machines. That is why wind farms are usually built in remote areas—in the desert, for example. The group says wind turbines don't belong in a fast-growing region that already includes 800 homes.

The preservation group admits that the wind farm would generate income for people who rent land for the towers. However, its members feel that it will mean economic loss for others. They say that the presence of wind turbines will lower the value of homes in the area. Because of the problems the wind farm will cause, people will not want to buy homes and farms in the township. The town will stop growing.

A number of other matters concern the members of the preservation group. Noise is sure to be a big problem, they say. The larger the turbine, the more air passes over the blades and the higher the noise level. To find out how much noise the turbines might make, group members spoke to people in communities where there are wind farms.

Residents of these areas reported that there is a deep "thump" each time a blade passes the turbine tower. One compared it to the pounding bass notes of a rock song at a neighbor's noisy party—a sound that can be both heard and felt. Others said the turbines sound like the "chop-chop" of helicopters in the distance.

Light is another concern. The rays of the sun bounce off the whirling turbine blades, flashing like strobe lights. Some wind farm neighbors complain that the light is even more irritating than the noise.

Opponents of the wind farm point out that the project will produce less than 1 percent of Wisconsin's total electricity.

Wisconsin's harsh winters and stormy summers raise weather-related worries, too. There are concerns that ice could form on the turbine blades in winter. The spinning blades would then hurl chunks of ice into the air. This could endanger nearby residents and their homes. Some people also wonder if the wind towers will be able to withstand the force of fierce thunderstorms and occasional tornadoes.

Many members of the preservation group think there is an even more significant worry. They fear that the worst thing about the wind farm is something that cannot be seen or heard. Invisible **electromagnetic fields** occur near electric power plants. Some medical studies suggest that people living close to electric power plants suffer from higher rates of cancer due to these fields. Other studies do not support this claim. People who oppose the wind farm feel that more research must be done to prove that electromagnetic fields do not harm humans.

Opponents of the wind farm point out that the project will produce less than 1 percent of Wisconsin's total electricity. Hardly enough, they feel, to justify taking any risk—no matter how small—with their lives or the lives of their children.

Glossary

abolish do away with, end

biodiversity variety of life forms that exist

census periodic count of a population

commuter person who travels some distance from home to work

conservation careful use to prevent waste and to preserve resources

continental U.S. all of the states except for Alaska and Hawaii

diversity variety

economy production, distribution, and use of goods and services

ecosystem community of living things

electromagnetic field area of electric waves

environment natural surroundings

extinct no longer existing or living

habitat environment where an animal normally lives, such as a forest or desert

industrial park an area, usually on the outskirts of a city, set aside for factories and other businesses

livestock domestic animals such as cattle and sheep

natural resources things supplied by nature, such as land, water, air, plants, and animals

platform the issues for which a person or group stands

rural relating to the country

suburb community close to a city

turbine engine powered by a stream of water, steam, or air

urban relating to a city

utility public service such as water, electricity, or garbage collection

Index